Silly Stories

This book of silly stories belongs to

Jonathan   miles

Silly Stories

Written by
Andy Charman, Heather Henning, Beatrice Phillpotts,
Caroline Repchuk, Louisa Somerville and Christine Tagg

Illustrated by
Diana Catchpole, Robin Edmonds, Chris Forsey
and Claire Mumford

This is a Parragon Book
This edition published in 2003

Parragon
Queen Street House
4 Queen Street
Bath BA1 1HE

Produced by
The Templar Company plc

Designed by Caroline Reeves

Printed and bound in China
ISBN 1-40542-033-2

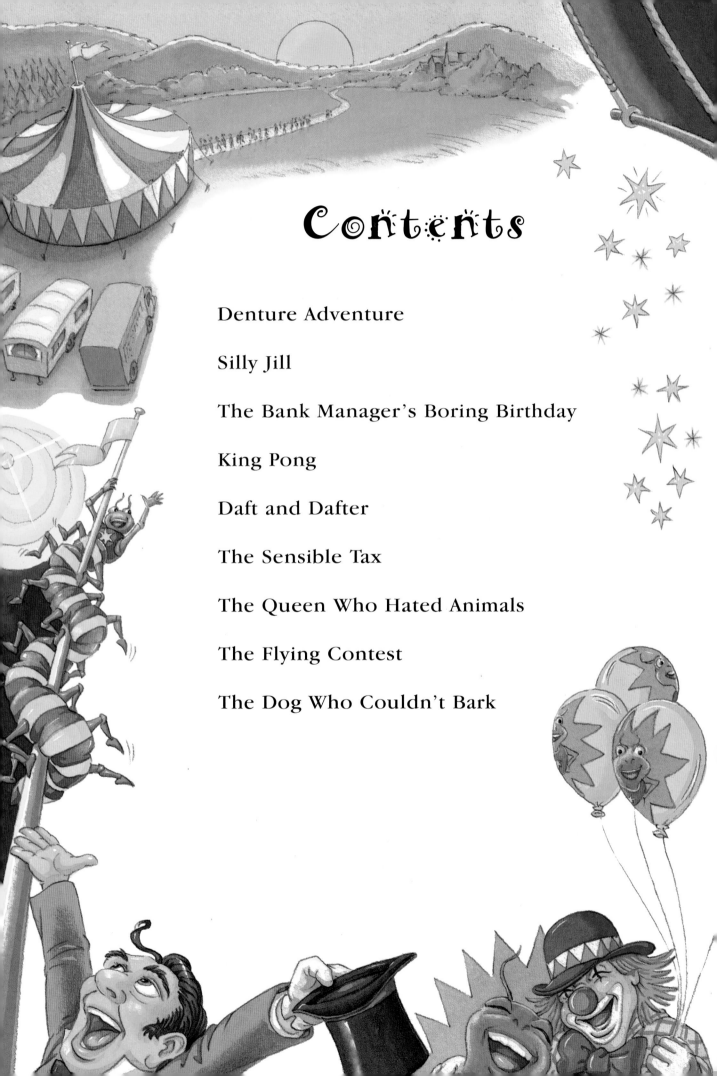

Contents

Denture Adventure

Grandad's teeth grinned broadly as they sat in the glass on the bedside table, next to his spectacles and a dish full of peanuts. Grandad snored while a large African Grey Parrot sat on the brass bedstead directly above Grandad's head. At precisely seven thirty it opened its beak and screeched, "Wakey, wakey," very, very loudly. Grandad stretched out his hand and, without opening his eyes, patted the parrot on the head. The parrot was quiet for exactly nine minutes and then he began again.

"Wakey, wakey," he called in a deafening screech. This continued until seven fifty seven when Grandad sat up in bed, yawned a gummy yawn and handed the parrot a peanut.

Grandad stumbled out of bed, put on his slippers and tripped across the hall to the bathroom. A face not unlike that of a turtle gazed back at him from the mirror, a turtle in Grandad's striped pyjamas. "Oh dear, oh dear," he said, gazing at his curious reflection. "Better put my teeth in."

Back in Grandad's bedroom, Norman the African Grey parrot had similar thoughts and was sitting proudly on the bedstead sporting Grandad's false teeth, which he had helped himself to from the glass whilst Grandad had been in the bathroom.

"Who's a pretty boy then?" he screeched

and the teeth fell out and dropped down behind the bed.

"Oh bother," said Grandad fishing around for them with the end of his best walking stick. But the teeth seemed to have vanished into thin air.

Grandma was in the kitchen making a large apple pie for tea.

"They can't have gone far," she said, as Grandad explained what had happened and, wiping her floury arms on her flowery apron, she climbed up the stairs to help him look.

"Men never look properly," she said getting down on both knees and reaching as far as she could under the big brass bed. She pulled out an old stripy sock with a hole in the toe, a furry mint humbug and a Christmas card from Auntie Beryl.

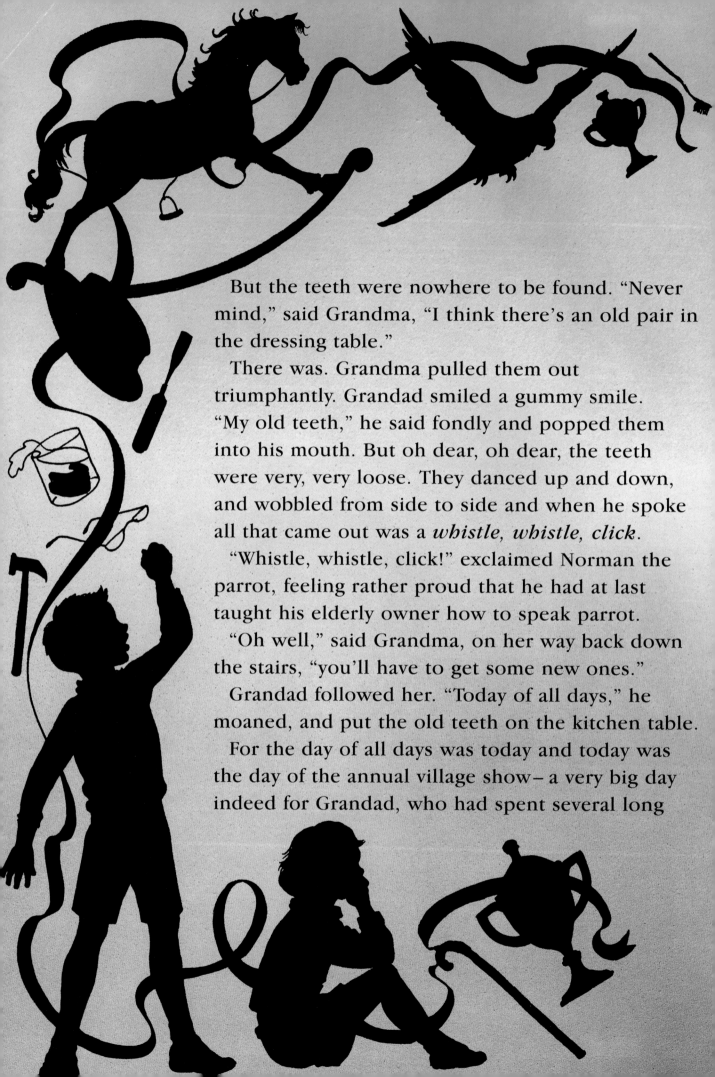

But the teeth were nowhere to be found. "Never mind," said Grandma, "I think there's an old pair in the dressing table."

There was. Grandma pulled them out triumphantly. Grandad smiled a gummy smile. "My old teeth," he said fondly and popped them into his mouth. But oh dear, oh dear, the teeth were very, very loose. They danced up and down, and wobbled from side to side and when he spoke all that came out was a *whistle, whistle, click*.

"Whistle, whistle, click!" exclaimed Norman the parrot, feeling rather proud that he had at last taught his elderly owner how to speak parrot.

"Oh well," said Grandma, on her way back down the stairs, "you'll have to get some new ones."

Grandad followed her. "Today of all days," he moaned, and put the old teeth on the kitchen table.

For the day of all days was today and today was the day of the annual village show – a very big day indeed for Grandad, who had spent several long

months making a magnificent rocking horse which he had entered in one of the craft classes.

"You'll just have to not smile today," suggested Grandma not very helpfully as she lay a large pastry blanket over the fat wedges of juicy apple. "Or talk," she added. Grandad shrugged his narrow shoulders and ambled over to his potting shed, feeling rather sorry for himself.

"Hmm, I wonder," said Grandma as she gazed at the false teeth sitting on the edge of her table. She picked them up thoughtfully and then very carefully and very neatly, she crimped the edge of her apple pie with them. Grandad stood in his shed flicking a duster over the shiny dappled neck of a fine rocking horse. He stood back to admire his work. The horse was perfect in every detail. A real leather saddle and bridle, a silken mane and tail, neat glossy black hooves and two large brown eyes with wonderful long lashes. Grandad rubbed his bristly chin and frowned.

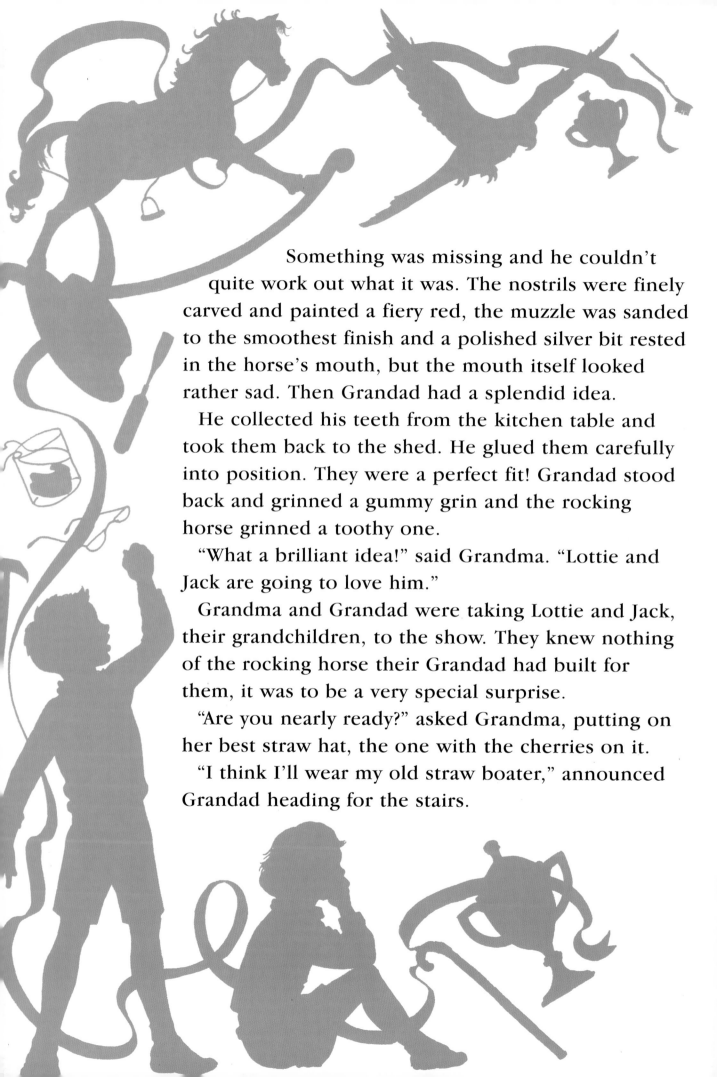

Something was missing and he couldn't quite work out what it was. The nostrils were finely carved and painted a fiery red, the muzzle was sanded to the smoothest finish and a polished silver bit rested in the horse's mouth, but the mouth itself looked rather sad. Then Grandad had a splendid idea.

He collected his teeth from the kitchen table and took them back to the shed. He glued them carefully into position. They were a perfect fit! Grandad stood back and grinned a gummy grin and the rocking horse grinned a toothy one.

"What a brilliant idea!" said Grandma. "Lottie and Jack are going to love him."

Grandma and Grandad were taking Lottie and Jack, their grandchildren, to the show. They knew nothing of the rocking horse their Grandad had built for them, it was to be a very special surprise.

"Are you nearly ready?" asked Grandma, putting on her best straw hat, the one with the cherries on it.

"I think I'll wear my old straw boater," announced Grandad heading for the stairs.

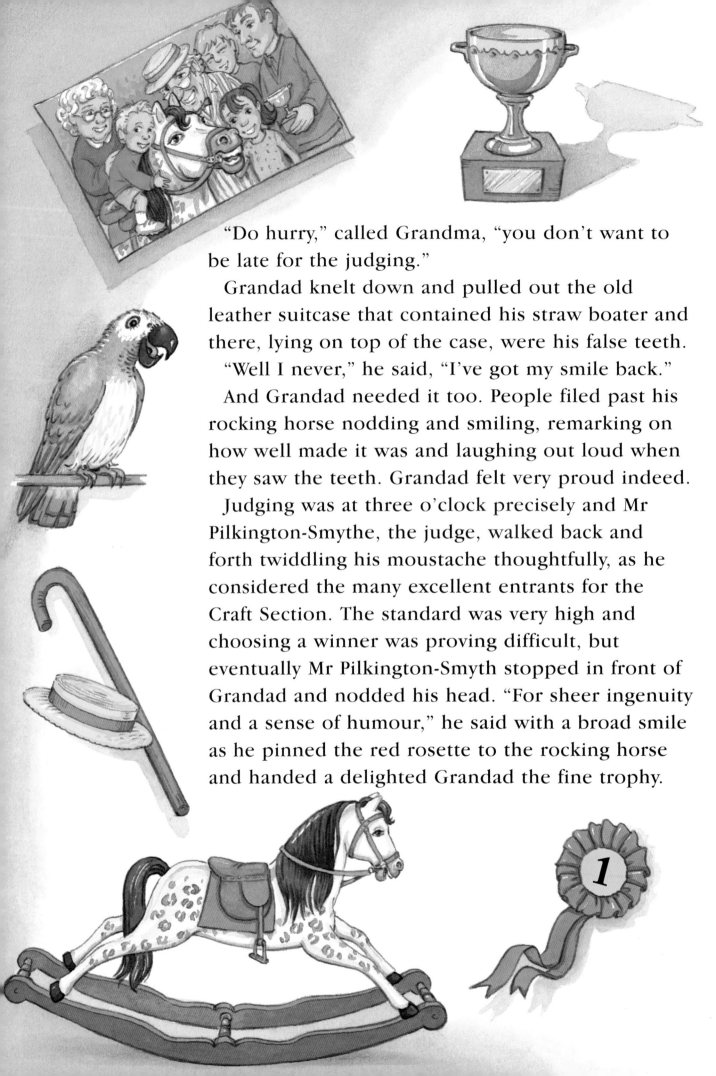

"Do hurry," called Grandma, "you don't want to be late for the judging."

Grandad knelt down and pulled out the old leather suitcase that contained his straw boater and there, lying on top of the case, were his false teeth.

"Well I never," he said, "I've got my smile back."

And Grandad needed it too. People filed past his rocking horse nodding and smiling, remarking on how well made it was and laughing out loud when they saw the teeth. Grandad felt very proud indeed.

Judging was at three o'clock precisely and Mr Pilkington-Smythe, the judge, walked back and forth twiddling his moustache thoughtfully, as he considered the many excellent entrants for the Craft Section. The standard was very high and choosing a winner was proving difficult, but eventually Mr Pilkington-Smyth stopped in front of Grandad and nodded his head. "For sheer ingenuity and a sense of humour," he said with a broad smile as he pinned the red rosette to the rocking horse and handed a delighted Grandad the fine trophy.

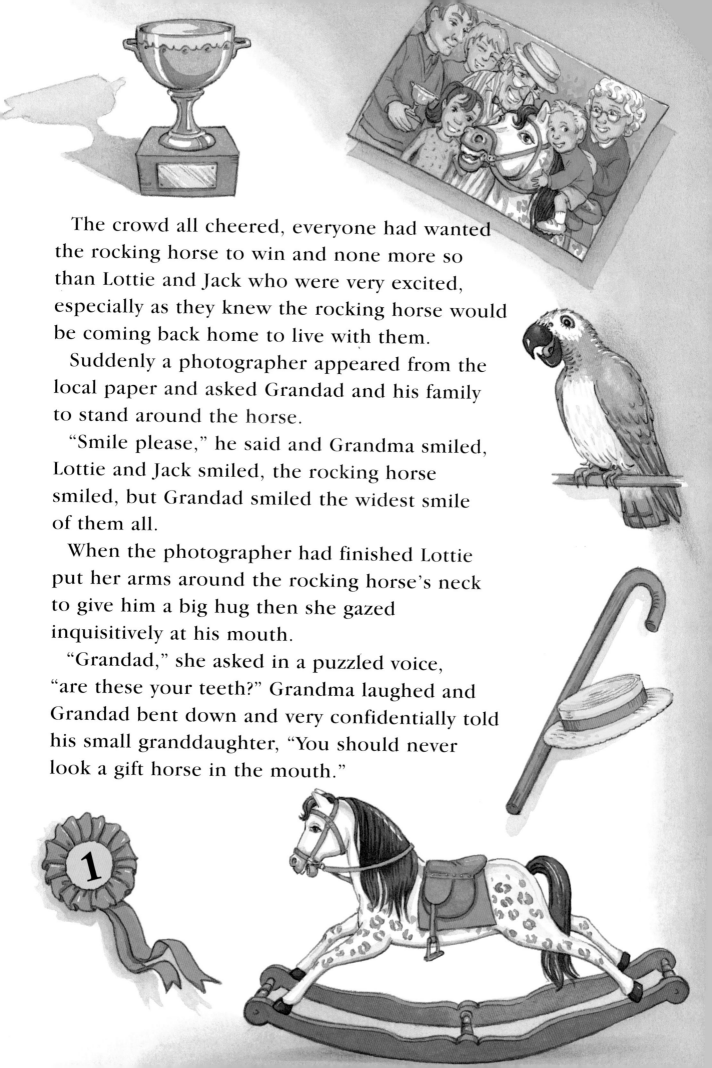

The crowd all cheered, everyone had wanted the rocking horse to win and none more so than Lottie and Jack who were very excited, especially as they knew the rocking horse would be coming back home to live with them.

Suddenly a photographer appeared from the local paper and asked Grandad and his family to stand around the horse.

"Smile please," he said and Grandma smiled, Lottie and Jack smiled, the rocking horse smiled, but Grandad smiled the widest smile of them all.

When the photographer had finished Lottie put her arms around the rocking horse's neck to give him a big hug then she gazed inquisitively at his mouth.

"Grandad," she asked in a puzzled voice, "are these your teeth?" Grandma laughed and Grandad bent down and very confidentially told his small granddaughter, "You should never look a gift horse in the mouth."

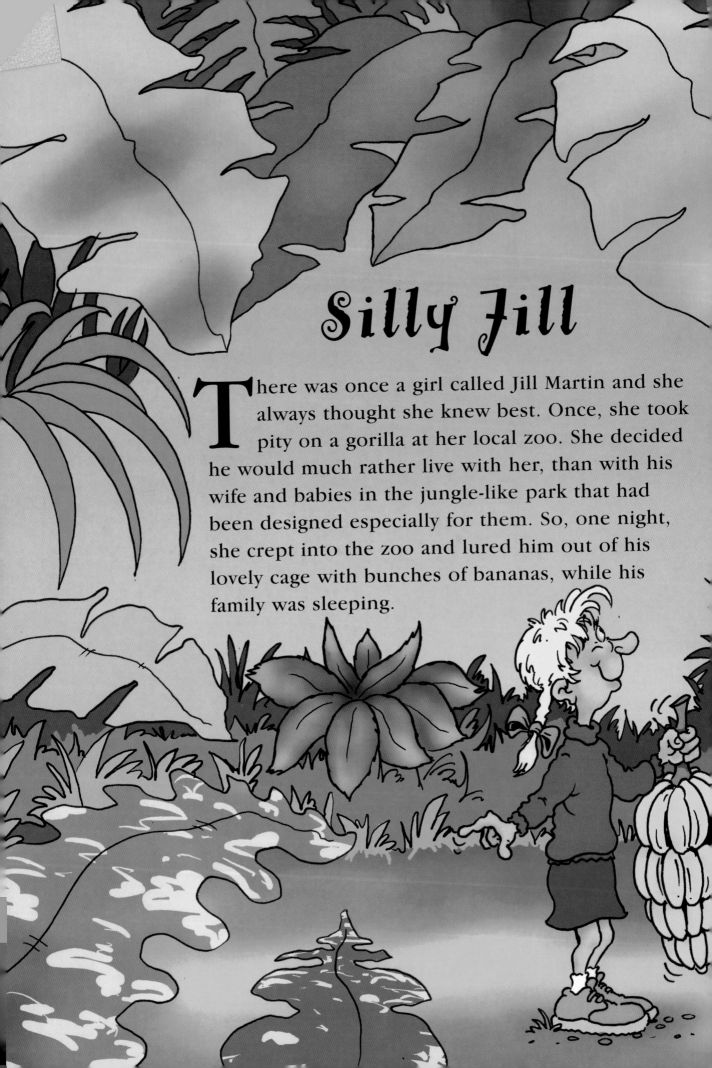

Silly Jill

There was once a girl called Jill Martin and she always thought she knew best. Once, she took pity on a gorilla at her local zoo. She decided he would much rather live with her, than with his wife and babies in the jungle-like park that had been designed especially for them. So, one night, she crept into the zoo and lured him out of his lovely cage with bunches of bananas, while his family was sleeping.

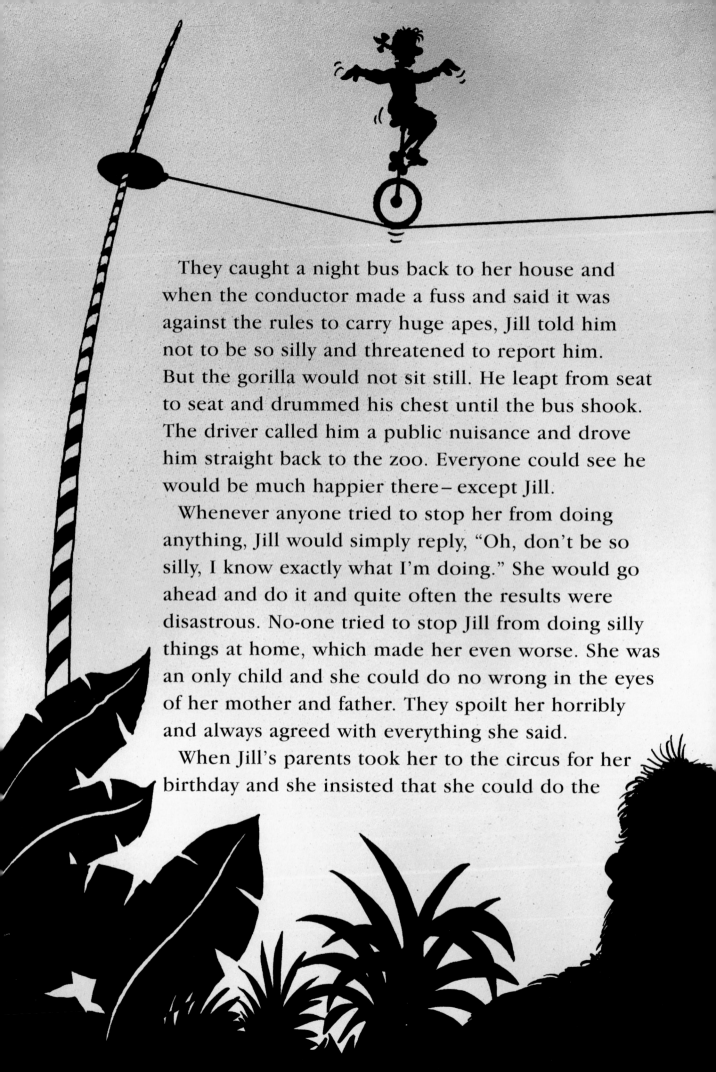

They caught a night bus back to her house and when the conductor made a fuss and said it was against the rules to carry huge apes, Jill told him not to be so silly and threatened to report him. But the gorilla would not sit still. He leapt from seat to seat and drummed his chest until the bus shook. The driver called him a public nuisance and drove him straight back to the zoo. Everyone could see he would be much happier there – except Jill.

Whenever anyone tried to stop her from doing anything, Jill would simply reply, "Oh, don't be so silly, I know exactly what I'm doing." She would go ahead and do it and quite often the results were disastrous. No-one tried to stop Jill from doing silly things at home, which made her even worse. She was an only child and she could do no wrong in the eyes of her mother and father. They spoilt her horribly and always agreed with everything she said.

When Jill's parents took her to the circus for her birthday and she insisted that she could do the

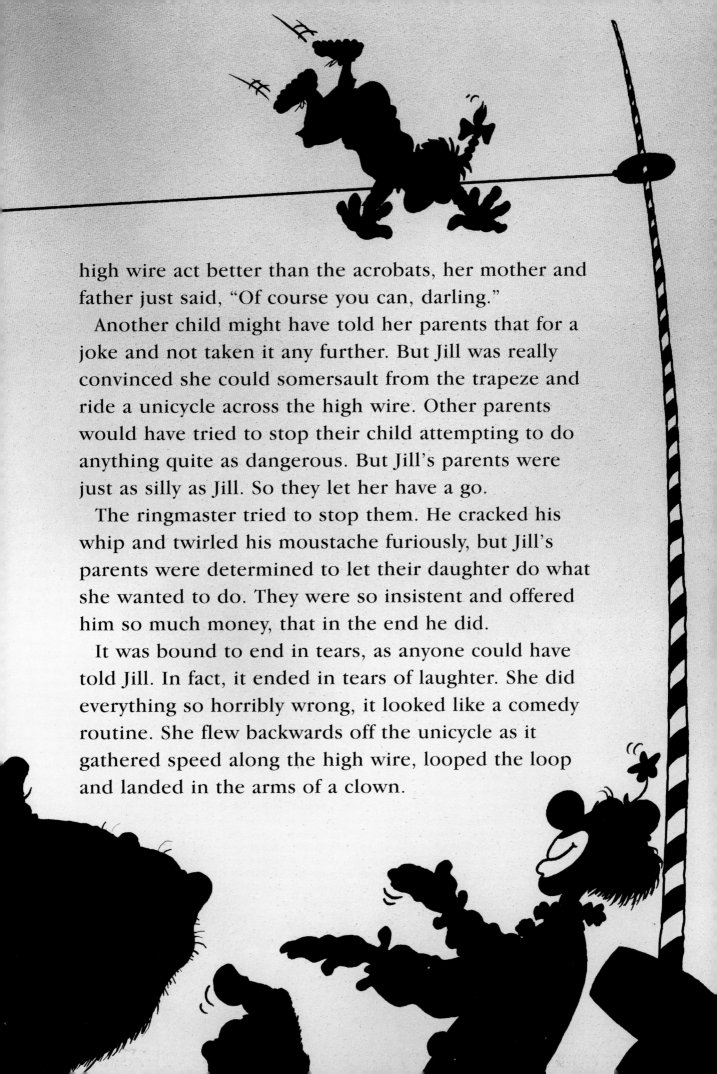

high wire act better than the acrobats, her mother and father just said, "Of course you can, darling."

Another child might have told her parents that for a joke and not taken it any further. But Jill was really convinced she could somersault from the trapeze and ride a unicycle across the high wire. Other parents would have tried to stop their child attempting to do anything quite as dangerous. But Jill's parents were just as silly as Jill. So they let her have a go.

The ringmaster tried to stop them. He cracked his whip and twirled his moustache furiously, but Jill's parents were determined to let their daughter do what she wanted to do. They were so insistent and offered him so much money, that in the end he did.

It was bound to end in tears, as anyone could have told Jill. In fact, it ended in tears of laughter. She did everything so horribly wrong, it looked like a comedy routine. She flew backwards off the unicycle as it gathered speed along the high wire, looped the loop and landed in the arms of a clown.

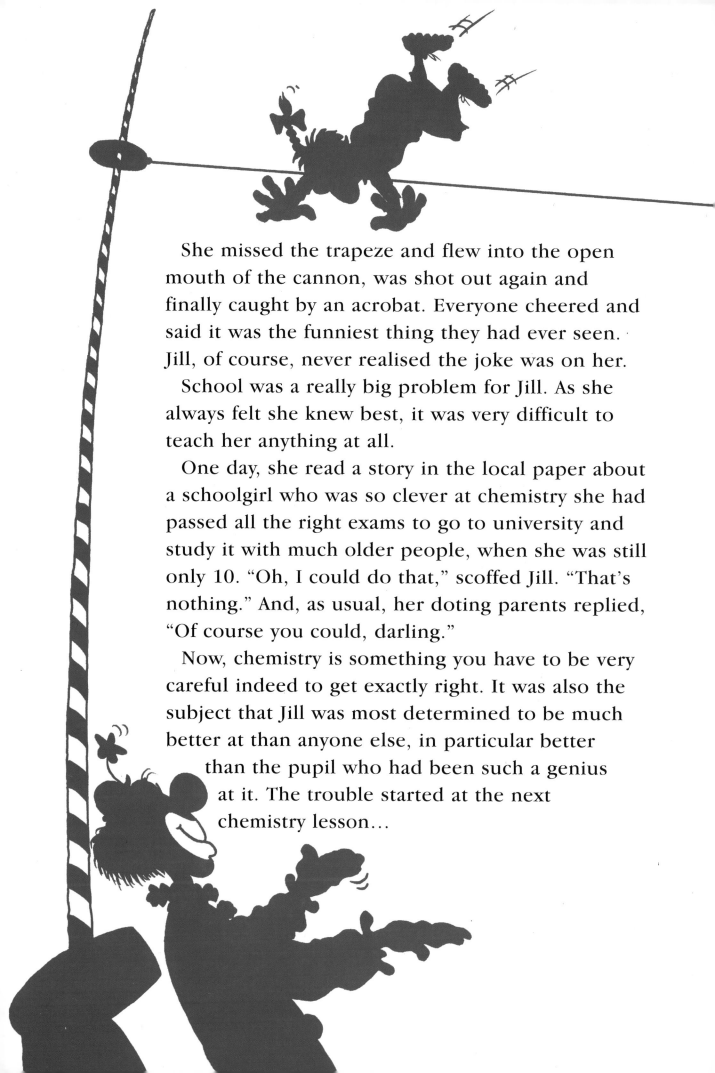

She missed the trapeze and flew into the open mouth of the cannon, was shot out again and finally caught by an acrobat. Everyone cheered and said it was the funniest thing they had ever seen. Jill, of course, never realised the joke was on her.

School was a really big problem for Jill. As she always felt she knew best, it was very difficult to teach her anything at all.

One day, she read a story in the local paper about a schoolgirl who was so clever at chemistry she had passed all the right exams to go to university and study it with much older people, when she was still only 10. "Oh, I could do that," scoffed Jill. "That's nothing." And, as usual, her doting parents replied, "Of course you could, darling."

Now, chemistry is something you have to be very careful indeed to get exactly right. It was also the subject that Jill was most determined to be much better at than anyone else, in particular better than the pupil who had been such a genius at it. The trouble started at the next chemistry lesson…

The rest of the class listened carefully to the chemistry teacher. She explained that in their next experiment it was very important not to mix the wrong liquids. Under no circumstances should blue be mixed with red.

'Huh!' thought Jill. 'I bet it works much better if you mix the blue with the red.' And so, without anyone seeing, she mixed blue and red.

Bang! Jill's flask exploded the moment they were combined and a stream of foul-smelling, smoking purple liquid poured onto the carpet.

"You silly, silly girl!" shouted the chemistry teacher. "What have you done?"

It was difficult to see exactly what Jill had done, the classroom was so full of smoke.

But everyone started to feel what she had done almost immediately.

"Help!" they shouted, as one by one, they felt themselves being lifted off the floor.

A most extraordinary thing had happened. The spilt liquid had made the pile of the carpet grow like grass. Only, instead of growing slowly like grass normally does, the carpet was growing upwards in leaps and bounds, like a meadow that had gone mad.

"Make for the door!" screamed the chemistry teacher, as the long waving pile of the classroom carpet carried them all up towards the ceiling. It was rather like being on a rollercoaster.

So they all did, even Jill. They crawled across the narrow space that was still left as fast as they could, trying not to knock their heads on the lights, while the whole carpet shot upwards in a great mass.

Then, just before they reached the door, the carpet flowered. Fat buds burst out into brightly coloured blooms. Everyone who suffered from hay fever, spluttered and sneezed.

Luckily, the classroom door was open. They squeezed their way through it before the carpet filled the room and then tumbled out into the corridor, chasing the last pupils out of the door.

"Run for it!" commanded the teacher, pressing the fire alarm to alert the rest of the school. And eight hundred pupils, including Jill, thirty members of staff, the caretaker and the cat raced for the safety of the playground, just before the school was completely swallowed up by carpet.

It took every fireman in the town a week to cut the carpet down and for months afterwards it still sprouted the occasional flower.

The school had to be closed, of course, while the giant carpet was scythed, mowed, rolled and finally brought under control. The head teacher was furious with Jill, when she heard how it had all started.

"Your silly, thoughtless behaviour could have destroyed my school and everyone in it," she told her. "I hope this has taught you a lesson and you know now that you do not always know better than anyone else."

Fortunately for Jill – and the school – it had taught her a lesson that she never forgot. From that dreadful day onwards, she stopped insisting she knew best and to everyone's relief, there were no more disasters.

In fact, Jill's terrible mistake turned out to be a fantastic opportunity for the school. An army chief heard about Jill's silly experiment and the amazing result. He decided that a quick-growing carpet would be an excellent weapon. He paid the school a lot of money for the details of Jill's purple mixture. This meant that the school was able to build a swimming pool, ice rink and bowling centre for everyone in the town. And it wasn't long before Jill mended her ways and really did become a star pupil – but everyone still knew her as Silly Jill!

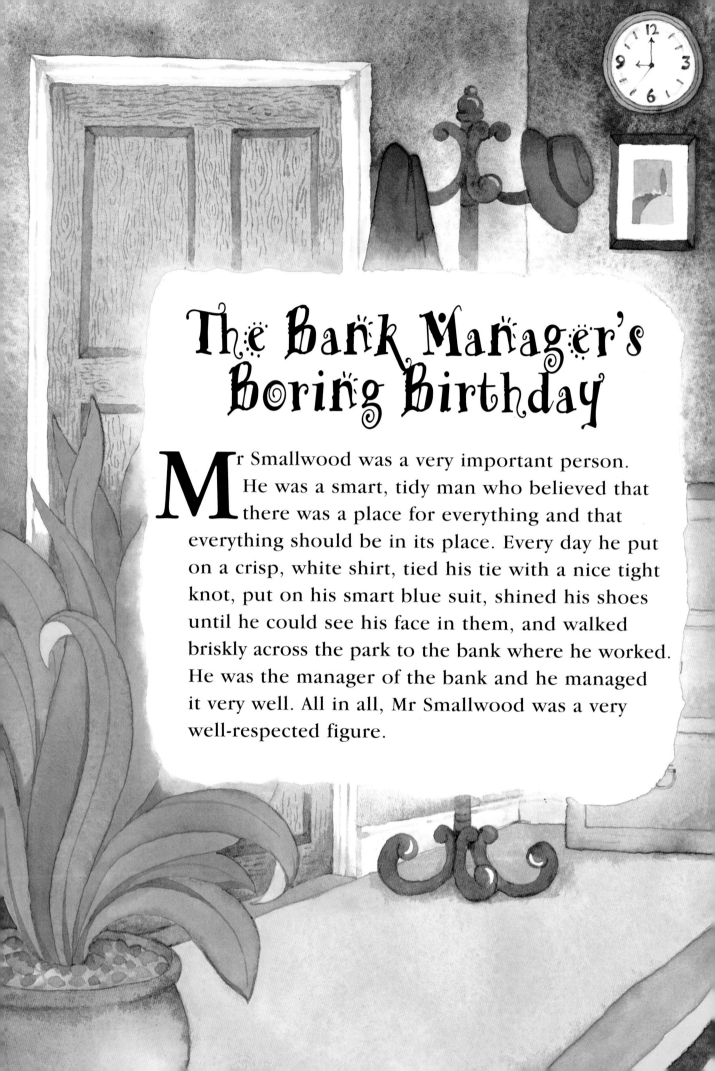

The Bank Manager's Boring Birthday

Mr Smallwood was a very important person. He was a smart, tidy man who believed that there was a place for everything and that everything should be in its place. Every day he put on a crisp, white shirt, tied his tie with a nice tight knot, put on his smart blue suit, shined his shoes until he could see his face in them, and walked briskly across the park to the bank where he worked. He was the manager of the bank and he managed it very well. All in all, Mr Smallwood was a very well-respected figure.

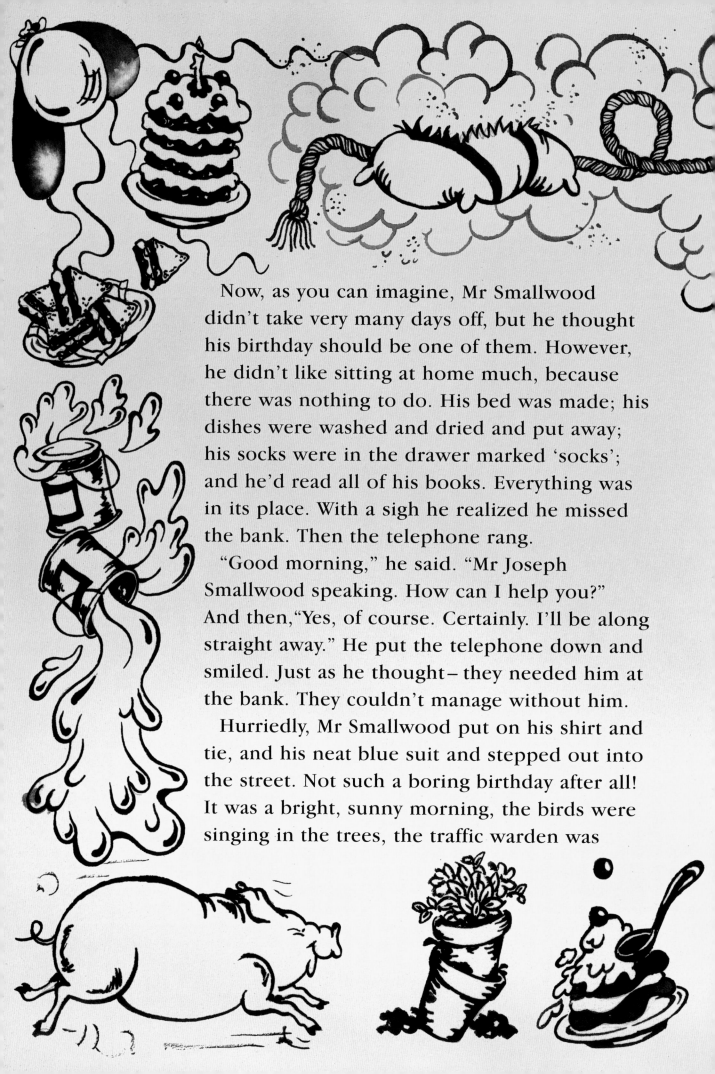

Now, as you can imagine, Mr Smallwood
didn't take very many days off, but he thought
his birthday should be one of them. However,
he didn't like sitting at home much, because
there was nothing to do. His bed was made; his
dishes were washed and dried and put away;
his socks were in the drawer marked 'socks';
and he'd read all of his books. Everything was
in its place. With a sigh he realized he missed
the bank. Then the telephone rang.

"Good morning," he said. "Mr Joseph
Smallwood speaking. How can I help you?"
And then,"Yes, of course. Certainly. I'll be along
straight away." He put the telephone down and
smiled. Just as he thought– they needed him at
the bank. They couldn't manage without him.

Hurriedly, Mr Smallwood put on his shirt and
tie, and his neat blue suit and stepped out into
the street. Not such a boring birthday after all!
It was a bright, sunny morning, the birds were
singing in the trees, the traffic warden was

writing tickets, the cars were at a standstill.
Everything was as it should be. A perfectly
ordinary day.

Mr Smallwood hadn't gone far when he came
across a pig.

"Now that's not the right place for a pig,"
said Mr Smallwood. "I should catch that
animal and take it to the market." So he chased
the pig into the park. But the pig had other
ideas. With an excited squeal, it dashed off to
hide in the rose bushes. Mr Smallwood
made a daring leap. He flew gracefully through
the air and stretching out his arms he caught the
pig. Then with a loud THWUMP! they landed in
a large, smelly heap of horse manure.

"Golly!" said Mr Smallwood, as he stood up.
The front of his suit and his glasses were
covered with horse manure, but the pig was
safely in his arms.

Mr Smallwood set off rather slowly across
the park in the direction of the market.

Now it may have been because he was distracted by the struggling pig, or it may have been because he couldn't see very well, but he didn't see the stack of paint cans outside the library until it was too late. CRASH! went the cans and down fell Mr Smallwood and the pig into a tide of canary-yellow paint.

Mr Smallwood stood up. There was paint all over his glasses and he could see hardly anything, but he couldn't wipe his glasses because he was still trying to keep hold of the pig. He struggled on, after all he was not a man to give up easily.

He hadn't gone far along the pavement when BUMP! he walked into a stand outside the florist's. Flowerpots and plants tumbled to the ground, breaking into a thousand pieces that tinkled around his feet. But one pot didn't break. As it fell, it turned over gracefully and landed right on top of Mr Smallwood's head.

"Gosh," cried Mr Smallwood, but even in the midst of this catastrophe, he still held onto the squealing pig.

Staggering somewhat and a little dazed, Mr Smallwood walked on. He hadn't gone very far when a voice cried, "LOOK OUT!" He walked straight into Claude, the waiter at the Crêpe Café. Claude was serving pancakes and ice cream to some customers, but they didn't get them. Down went Claude, up in the air went his tray, and SLAP! two pancakes landed squarely on Mr Smallwood's shiny shoes.

Always a polite man, Mr Smallwood turned to apologize to Claude and his customers. "Sorry!" he called out. But before he knew what was happening he was falling, stumbling backwards into a hole full of muddy water on a building site.

"Golly," said Mr Smallwood, and, still holding firmly onto the pig, he pulled himself out of the hole. Now, perhaps it was because he was tired by now and not concentrating, or perhaps it was because he had manure and paint and mud on his glasses, but Mr Smallwood didn't realize that he was on a building site. He also didn't realize that he was pulling himself up by a rope attached to a pile of cement bags. The pile swayed, the pile wobbled. The top bag slid off and exploded majestically over Mr Smallwood's head, covering him in a cloud of cement dust.

Mr Smallwood coughed, wheezed and spluttered as the cloud gradually cleared.

The cement began to harden as it soaked into Mr Smallwood's damp suit. He walked away, stiffly.

He hadn't gone far when he heard a familiar voice, and it was calling his name.

"Mr Smallwood! There you are! We were wondering where you'd got to." It was Mrs Tillhead, the assistant bank manager.

Tired and a little shaken, Mr Smallwood allowed himself to be led into the bank. As soon as he entered the building, a cheer went up.

"Hurrah," he heard, and "Happy Birthday!" Someone removed his glasses and cleaned them for him, and he looked around the room. The ceiling was hung with brightly coloured streamers and balloons.

Above the cash desks was a huge banner with the words 'HAPPY BIRTHDAY MR SMALLWOOD' and a table was bending under the weight of crisps, sandwiches and cakes. His staff had thrown a surprise birthday party for him!

Mr Smallwood was very surprised, but not as surprised as everyone else!

Instead of seeing the small, dapper bank manager they expected and respected, they saw in front of them a man walking stiffly in a cement-covered suit, with a flower pot on his head, pancakes draped over his shoes, smelling very strongly of horse manure and carrying a yellow, wriggling pig in his arms.

"Golly!" they cried.

King Pong

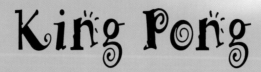

There once lived a king who was very fond of gardening. The royal garden was the talk of the kingdom, and the king spent most of his time tending the royal blooms. They were the most magnificent flowers you could ever imagine. There were vibrant violets, delicate delphiniums, marvellous marigolds and even lovely ruby red roses. The king could grow just about anything, and everyone said that he had green fingers, but this was largely due to the fact that he never washed his hands.

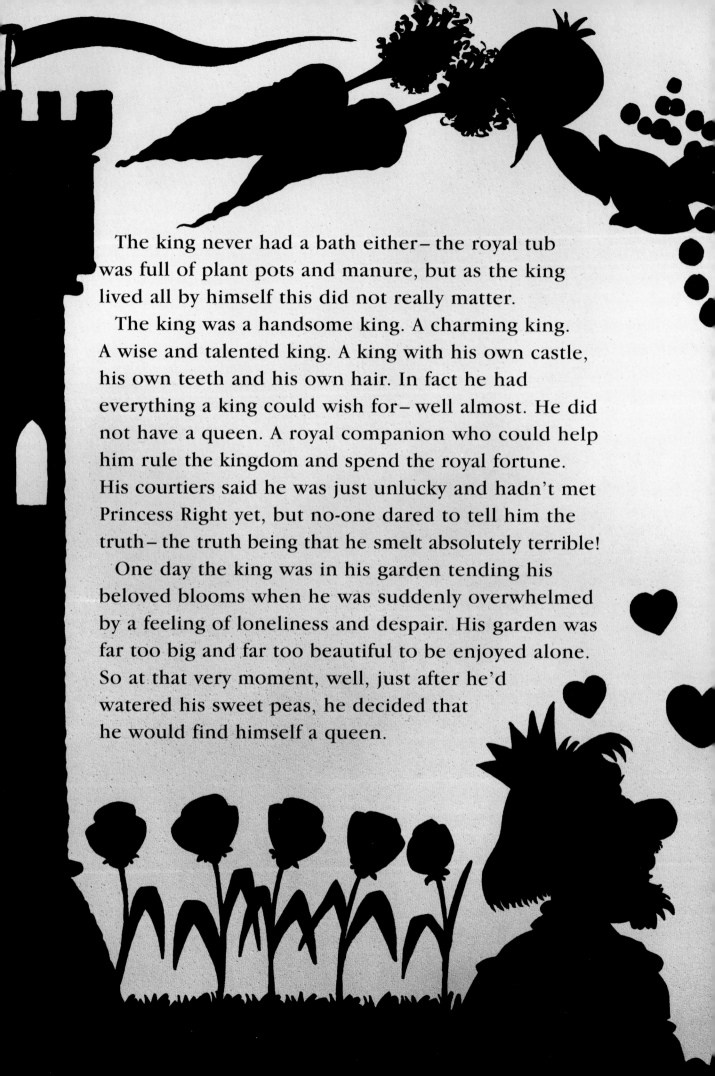

The king never had a bath either – the royal tub
was full of plant pots and manure, but as the king
lived all by himself this did not really matter.

The king was a handsome king. A charming king.
A wise and talented king. A king with his own castle,
his own teeth and his own hair. In fact he had
everything a king could wish for – well almost. He did
not have a queen. A royal companion who could help
him rule the kingdom and spend the royal fortune.
His courtiers said he was just unlucky and hadn't met
Princess Right yet, but no-one dared to tell him the
truth – the truth being that he smelt absolutely terrible!

One day the king was in his garden tending his
beloved blooms when he was suddenly overwhelmed
by a feeling of loneliness and despair. His garden was
far too big and far too beautiful to be enjoyed alone.
So at that very moment, well, just after he'd
watered his sweet peas, he decided that
he would find himself a queen.

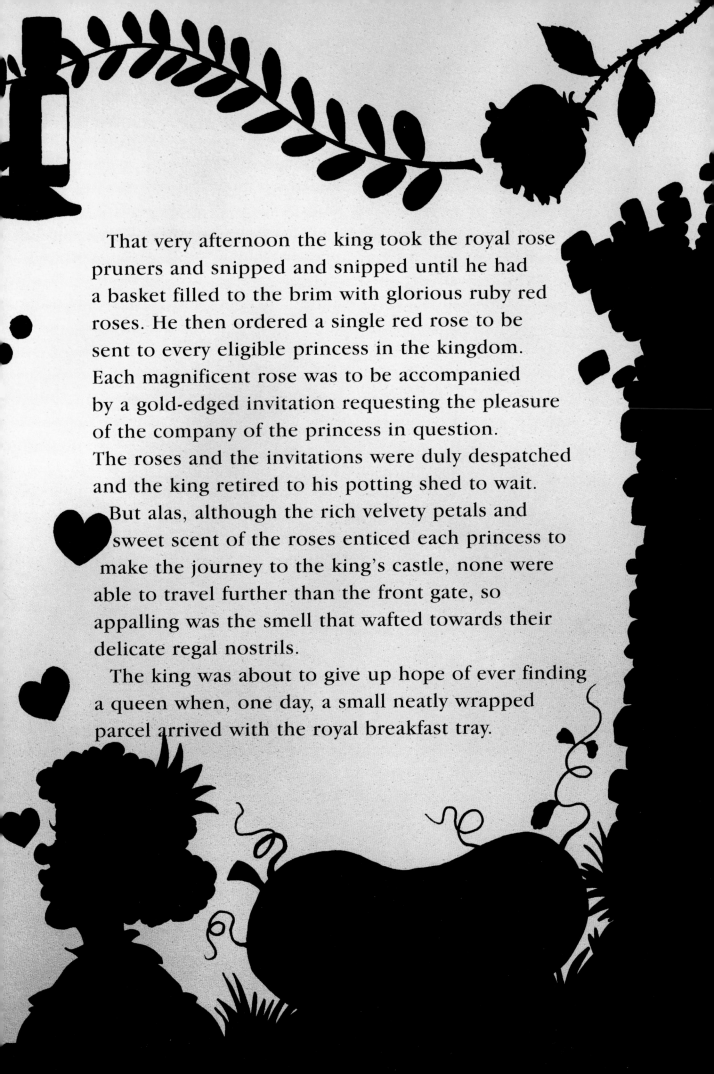

That very afternoon the king took the royal rose
pruners and snipped and snipped until he had
a basket filled to the brim with glorious ruby red
roses. He then ordered a single red rose to be
sent to every eligible princess in the kingdom.
Each magnificent rose was to be accompanied
by a gold-edged invitation requesting the pleasure
of the company of the princess in question.
The roses and the invitations were duly despatched
and the king retired to his potting shed to wait.

But alas, although the rich velvety petals and
sweet scent of the roses enticed each princess to
make the journey to the king's castle, none were
able to travel further than the front gate, so
appalling was the smell that wafted towards their
delicate regal nostrils.

The king was about to give up hope of ever finding
a queen when, one day, a small neatly wrapped
parcel arrived with the royal breakfast tray.

Inside was a tiny bottle of vibrant orange liquid and a short hand written note, which read:

Her Royal Highness regrets that she is unable to accept your invitation, but thanks you for the delightful rose, which did incidentally have a touch of greenfly. Her Royal Highness has therefore taken the liberty of enclosing an excellent preparation which should combat this.

The king was intrigued. The very next day he ordered that one dozen royal red roses, minus green fly, of course, be despatched directly to the princess with another invitation asking if she would join him for afternoon tea on Tuesday at four o'clock prompt.

The next morning the king received a large, neatly wrapped parcel containing a splendid Savoy cabbage and a short hand written note which read:

Her Royal Highness thanks you most sincerely for the generous bouquet and trusts that you will accept this cabbage as a token of her appreciation. Sadly she is unable to accept your offer of tea.

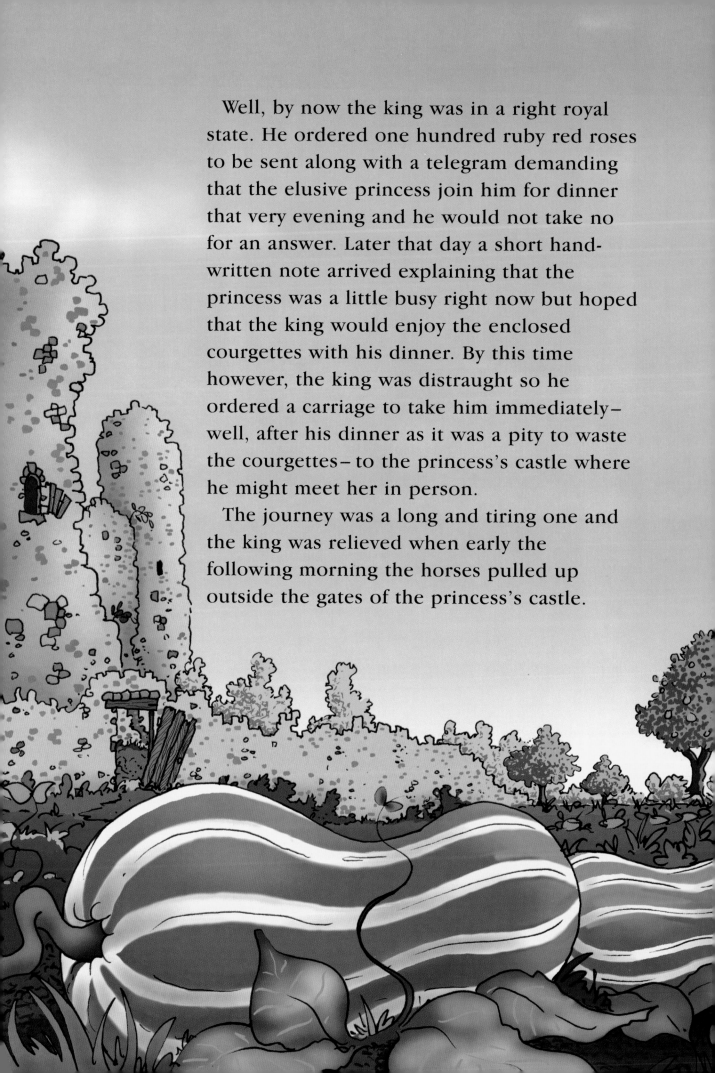

Well, by now the king was in a right royal state. He ordered one hundred ruby red roses to be sent along with a telegram demanding that the elusive princess join him for dinner that very evening and he would not take no for an answer. Later that day a short hand-written note arrived explaining that the princess was a little busy right now but hoped that the king would enjoy the enclosed courgettes with his dinner. By this time however, the king was distraught so he ordered a carriage to take him immediately – well, after his dinner as it was a pity to waste the courgettes – to the princess's castle where he might meet her in person.

The journey was a long and tiring one and the king was relieved when early the following morning the horses pulled up outside the gates of the princess's castle.

The king clambered out and gazed at the crumbling towers that held the crumbling walls of the castle together. It was very very run down. The gates were rusty and one was hanging off its hinges. Unperturbed the king walked up the uneven muddy driveway and knocked at the rotten front door of the castle. There was no reply, so he knocked again and he would have knocked a third time but the knocker came off in his hand so he decided to try round the back instead. He passed through a rickety wooden door set in an ancient moss-covered wall and found himself in the most fantastic vegetable garden he had ever seen.

There were marrows bigger than carriages, great fat pea pods ready to burst, cabbages, cauliflowers and lettuces all growing in perfectly straight lines and in such abundance it took your breath away.

At the far end of the garden he saw a figure effortlessly pulling up bunches of enormous juicy carrots and throwing them into the basket by her side. She was tall and very strong. Her hair was the colour of the carrots and hung in unruly curls about her grubby face. Her patched trousers were held up with string. She paused to wipe her nose on her sleeve and it was love at first sight. The king gave a little cough to attract her attention. The vision of loveliness looked up and the king walked steadily over to her, not noticing that she didn't smell particularly nice. He bowed politely and kissed her grimy hand. The princess blushed the colour of the wonderful beetroots that were sitting in her basket.

"I'm so glad you came," she said, offering him a radish. "It's been lonely since the staff left."

"You're very beautiful," the king told her and he meant it. The princess smiled a shy smile. "Oh you're just being nice," she said. "I'm afraid I've been so wrapped up in the garden I've rather neglected myself."

"Nonsense," said the king. "You are by far the prettiest flower in your garden."

"You are very kind," said the princess – who was far too polite to point out that she only grew vegetables.

The king then knelt in the slimy green mud to propose. Princess Composta, for that was her name, accepted without hesitation.

"We must be married at once," announced the king, and so they were – well, after he'd helped her dig up the spuds.

And they both lived smellily ever after.

Daft and Dafter

"Miaow!"

Tommy looked up at the faint sound of a kitten purring somewhere above his head. Then he blinked in amazement. The kitten was not stuck in a tree– it appeared to be floating down through the sky! Even more incredibly, other kittens were gently falling downwards. It couldn't be true! Were his eyes playing tricks? He looked up again. But it was true! And there were puppies floating down, as well!

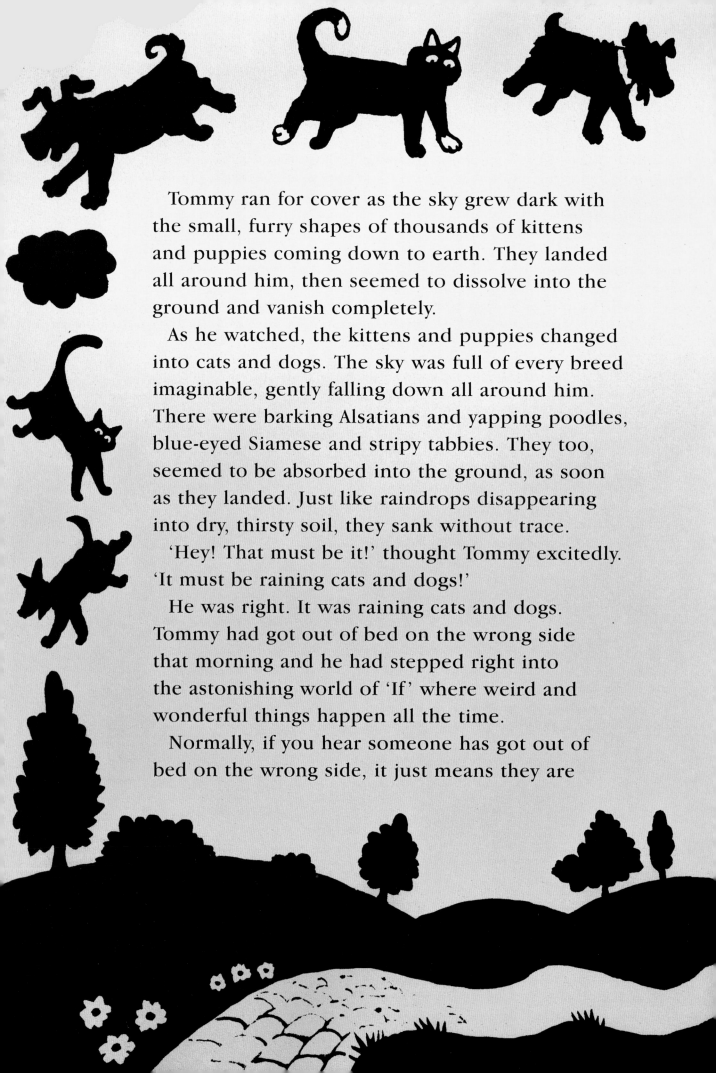

Tommy ran for cover as the sky grew dark with the small, furry shapes of thousands of kittens and puppies coming down to earth. They landed all around him, then seemed to dissolve into the ground and vanish completely.

As he watched, the kittens and puppies changed into cats and dogs. The sky was full of every breed imaginable, gently falling down all around him. There were barking Alsatians and yapping poodles, blue-eyed Siamese and stripy tabbies. They too, seemed to be absorbed into the ground, as soon as they landed. Just like raindrops disappearing into dry, thirsty soil, they sank without trace.

'Hey! That must be it!' thought Tommy excitedly. 'It must be raining cats and dogs!'

He was right. It was raining cats and dogs. Tommy had got out of bed on the wrong side that morning and he had stepped right into the astonishing world of 'If' where weird and wonderful things happen all the time.

Normally, if you hear someone has got out of bed on the wrong side, it just means they are

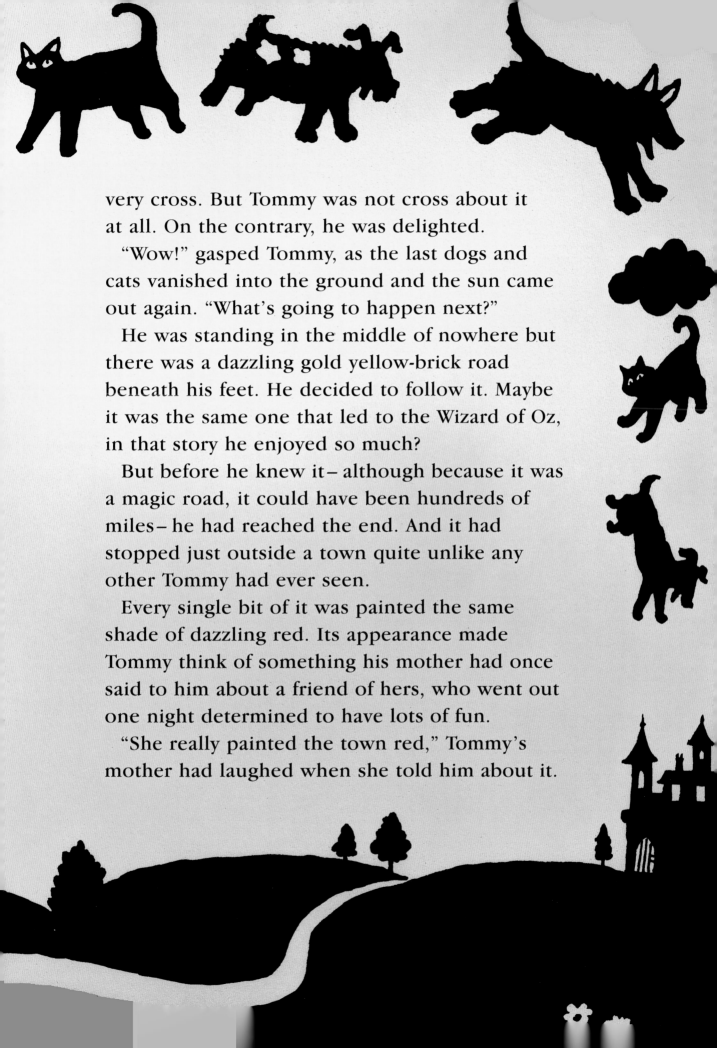

very cross. But Tommy was not cross about it at all. On the contrary, he was delighted.

"Wow!" gasped Tommy, as the last dogs and cats vanished into the ground and the sun came out again. "What's going to happen next?"

He was standing in the middle of nowhere but there was a dazzling gold yellow-brick road beneath his feet. He decided to follow it. Maybe it was the same one that led to the Wizard of Oz, in that story he enjoyed so much?

But before he knew it– although because it was a magic road, it could have been hundreds of miles– he had reached the end. And it had stopped just outside a town quite unlike any other Tommy had ever seen.

Every single bit of it was painted the same shade of dazzling red. Its appearance made Tommy think of something his mother had once said to him about a friend of hers, who went out one night determined to have lots of fun.

"She really painted the town red," Tommy's mother had laughed when she told him about it.

Tommy knew that meant she'd had a really good time, not that she'd spent the whole night with a paintbrush in her hand. That wouldn't have been much fun! Looking at this town, however, it looked as if someone had done precisely that.

The fact that absolutely everything, even the trees and flowers, were the same shade of red was not the only weird thing about the town. It also appeared to be completely deserted.

Or was it? Out of the corner of his eye, Tommy thought he saw moving figures. It was very spooky.

'This looks like a ghost town,' thought Tommy.

He was right. It was full of ghosts. But these ghosts were frightened of him!

"You're not going to haunt us, are you?" a friendly phantom plucked up courage to ask Tommy. "We've heard that humans go round wailing and clanking chains."

Tommy was about to reply, "No, that's what ghosts do!" but he realised that everything was back to front here. So he just smiled and said that of course he wouldn't.

However, Tommy was feeling a bit nervous himself and he was keen to explore the strange new world.

"I'm tired of seeing red," he told the phantom. "It's driving me up the wall."

His words came true. A moment later, Tommy found himself standing on the top of a great wall that went all around the town.

"I've been told that walls have ears," Tommy told it, jokingly. "Maybe you do! You are quite unlike any wall I've ever met."

"You needn't shout!" the wall retorted, proving that it did have excellent hearing.

Just then, a loud and very unexpected 'oink' sounded above Tommy's head, followed by a succession of noisy grunts. Tommy looked up and was amazed to see a herd of pigs flying towards him. They had made a V-shaped

formation, like geese, but squealed rather
than honked as they flew, propelling
themselves along by flapping their huge pink
ears.

"Well, if it can rain cats and dogs, there's no
reason why pigs shouldn't fly!" Tommy
laughed. "Maybe we could even hitch a ride
on the back of one."

"Come on!" he shouted to the friendly ghost.

They both rose to the occasion – in the
wonderful world of 'If', you really can – and
floated upwards to join the flying pigs.

"You want to go the whole hog, do you?"
squealed a large black-and-white sow with ten
spotted piglets fluttering along behind her.
"Well, jump aboard."

She flew them down to a beach and then
took off again.

"I must keep up with the others," she grunted. "Or they'll have my bacon."

Tommy and the ghost made for the inviting blue sea. Curiously, it seemed to be singing. As Tommy got closer, he realised it was the sound of many different singsong voices, all talking at once but very softly. He couldn't hear what they were saying to him, but it all sounded very flattering.

"I think they must be whispering sweet nothings to me," Tommy laughed.

"Whhoo-oo, I love sweet nothings!" the ghost moaned with pleasure. "I'll sit here for a bit and fish for compliments."

He produced a fishing net out of thin air and dipped it into the ocean. But all he got for his pains, was a sackful of trouble.

This being 'If', however, it was not an imaginary sack full of imaginary troubles, it was the real thing.

"We're in for the high jump now," Tommy said anxiously, fearing the worst, as the bulging bag was lifted out, dripping with water and looking like a real load of problems. He suddenly felt himself going up in the world again. But this time it was as if he was bouncing off an extra springy trampoline.

"We're not 'in for the high jump', we are in a high jump," Tommy called to the phantom delightedly.

But when he finally came down to earth again with a bump, there was no sign of the friendly ghost. In fact, he was right back where he had started – in bed.

And Tommy did wonder if he might not have dreamed the whole thing. Just in case, he quickly looked out of the window to see if it was still raining cats and dogs – but there was only a clear blue sky!

The Sensible Tax

"The bridge is falling down," said the Minister for Transport.

"We need more golf balls," said the Minister for Sport.

The Prime Minister didn't look up from his papers, but waved his hand wearily and said with a sigh, "Go to the Treasury, and get what you need."

"The Treasury is empty, Sir. There's not a single penny left."

"I don't believe it," said the Prime Minister. "It was full last week."

"I think we spent it all on that tunnel under the sea, Sir," said the second minister. "You know, the one we can't find the entrance to."

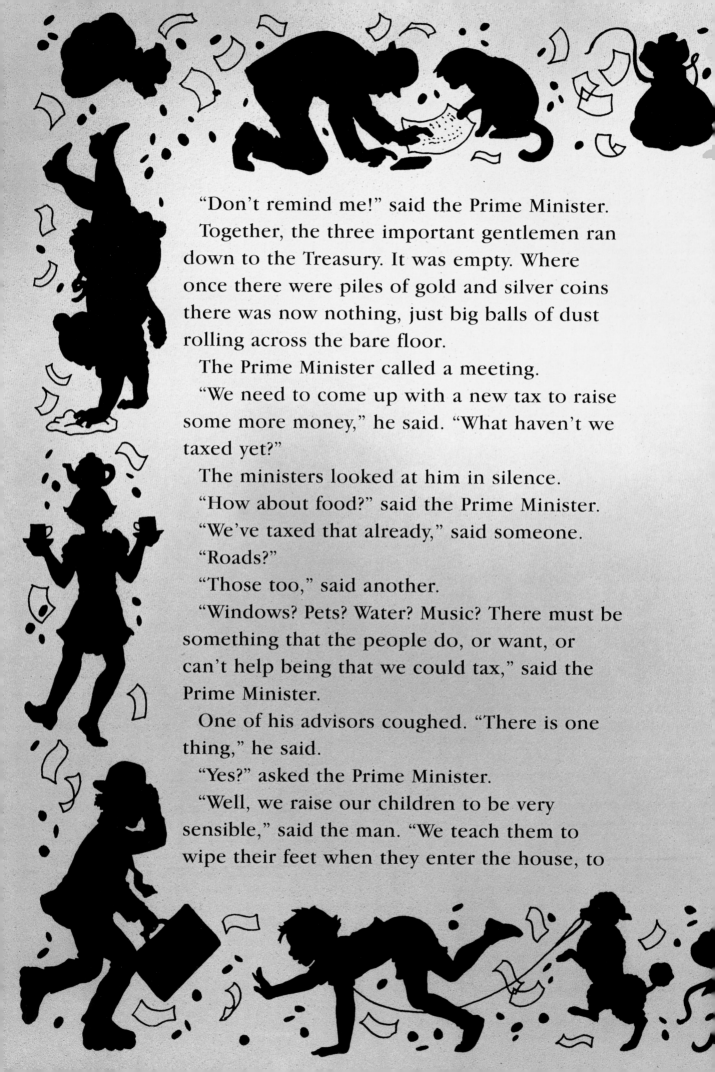

"Don't remind me!" said the Prime Minister.

Together, the three important gentlemen ran down to the Treasury. It was empty. Where once there were piles of gold and silver coins there was now nothing, just big balls of dust rolling across the bare floor.

The Prime Minister called a meeting.

"We need to come up with a new tax to raise some more money," he said. "What haven't we taxed yet?"

The ministers looked at him in silence.

"How about food?" said the Prime Minister.

"We've taxed that already," said someone.

"Roads?"

"Those too," said another.

"Windows? Pets? Water? Music? There must be something that the people do, or want, or can't help being that we could tax," said the Prime Minister.

One of his advisors coughed. "There is one thing," he said.

"Yes?" asked the Prime Minister.

"Well, we raise our children to be very sensible," said the man. "We teach them to wipe their feet when they enter the house, to brush their teeth before going to bed, not to wipe their noses on their sleeves..."

"Quite right," interrupted the Prime Minister.

"...This means that most people are sensible..."

"And we can tax them for it," said the Prime Minister. "That's brilliant."

So the Prime Minister introduced the Sensible Tax. Anyone who behaved sensibly would have to pay money to the Treasury. Tax officers were sent out to collect the money, and at first it was a great success.

They taxed people for getting to work on time, for carrying umbrellas if it looked as if it was going to rain. They taxed people for walking their dogs, for not eating snacks between meals, for riding on the bus if it was too far to walk.

Once the tax officers got used to the new tax, there seemed no end of things they could tax people for. At the football pitch they taxed every single player for kicking the ball towards the other team's goal, at the sports stadium they taxed all the runners for sprinting towards the finishing line. The Treasury soon began to fill up again.

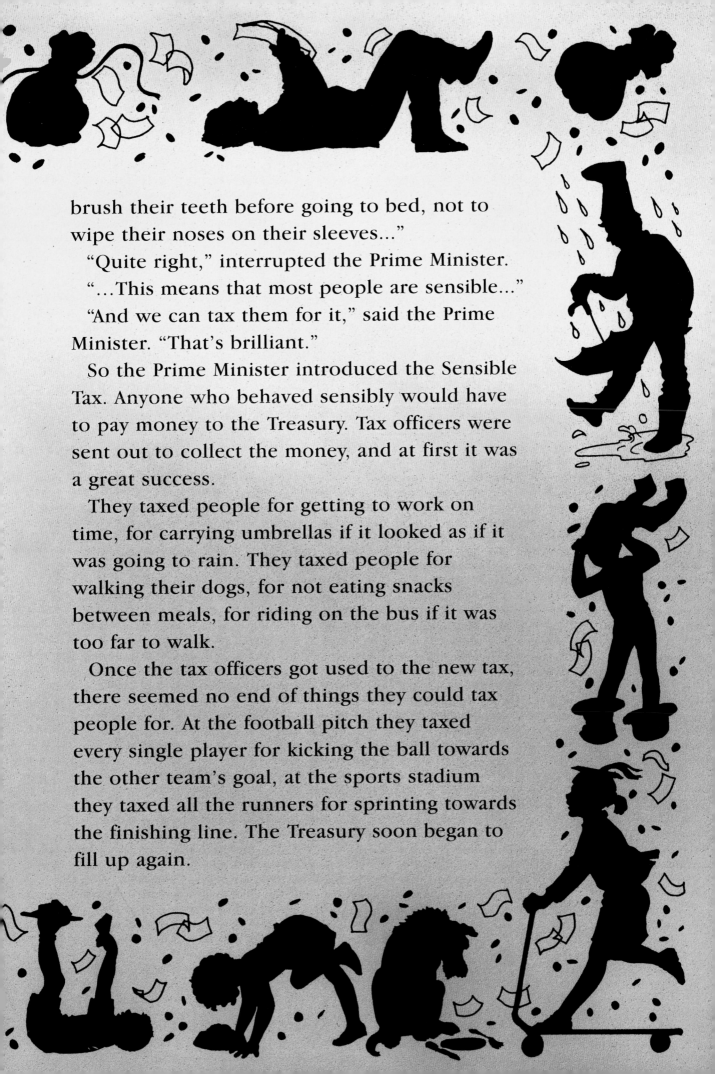

Of course, the new tax wasn't very popular with the people, and very soon they began to grumble.

"I've just been taxed for wearing my scarf," said Benjamin's dad when he came home from work one evening.

"Why were you wearing your scarf, George?" said his wife, Myrtle.

"Well, it's cold out," he asked.

"Yes, of course," she replied.

"This is ridiculous," said George. "All our lives we are told to be sensible and now they charge us for it. It's not a sensible tax, it's a completely stupid tax. The only people who never have to pay anything are those who are as daft as ducks."

Just then there was a knock at the door.

"I'm a tax officer," said the man at the door.

"This is just a random house check. Am I correct in thinking that you are about to eat dinner at dinner time, Madam?" said the man.

"Yes," said Myrtle.

"And is it piping hot and straight from the oven?" said the man.

"Yes," came the reply.

"And is it cooked all the way through? And will you be sitting at the dinner table to eat it, Madam? And is there pudding to follow?"

Myrtle answered 'yes' to all of these questions and the officer handed her a tax bill.

Just then Benjamin came wandering down the stairs wearing a wetsuit and a pair of flippers, and a top hat on his head.

"I don't want dinner," he said to his mum. "I've been eating chocolate all day. I'm off out now. I'll be back long after my bedtime."

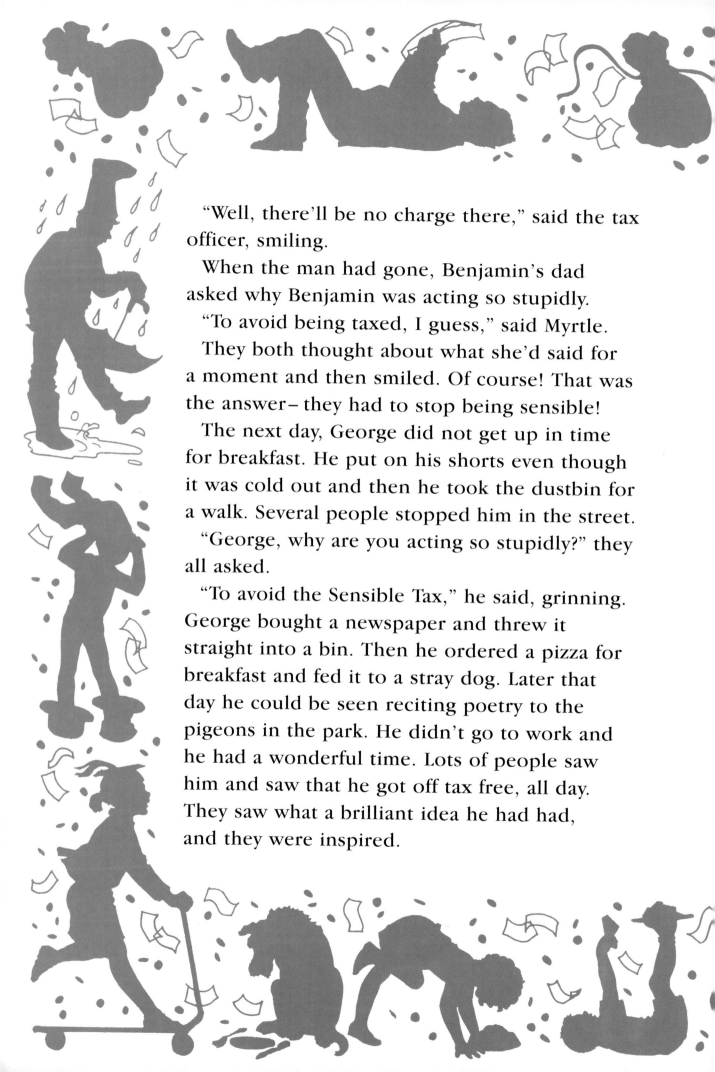

"Well, there'll be no charge there," said the tax officer, smiling.

When the man had gone, Benjamin's dad asked why Benjamin was acting so stupidly.

"To avoid being taxed, I guess," said Myrtle.

They both thought about what she'd said for a moment and then smiled. Of course! That was the answer – they had to stop being sensible!

The next day, George did not get up in time for breakfast. He put on his shorts even though it was cold out and then he took the dustbin for a walk. Several people stopped him in the street.

"George, why are you acting so stupidly?" they all asked.

"To avoid the Sensible Tax," he said, grinning. George bought a newspaper and threw it straight into a bin. Then he ordered a pizza for breakfast and fed it to a stray dog. Later that day he could be seen reciting poetry to the pigeons in the park. He didn't go to work and he had a wonderful time. Lots of people saw him and saw that he got off tax free, all day. They saw what a brilliant idea he had had, and they were inspired.

The next day, most people didn't go to work at all, and those who did didn't get there on time; some even went to the wrong jobs.

They walked if it was too far to walk; if they had bicycles, they carried them. A lot of people went to the cinema in the afternoon dressed as pirates, but they didn't watch the film. No, that would have been too sensible. They faced the other way and sang football songs at the tops of their voices, instead.

They all had a great day, and the next day they all got up late and did it all over again, only this time they found even more ways to be silly.

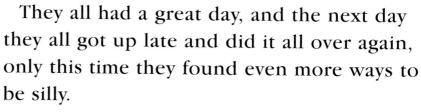

The tax officers began to look worried – the money had stopped coming in – and the ministers were even more worried. No-one was doing any work; the country was falling apart. They called an emergency meeting with the Prime Minister.

"Sorry I'm late," said the Prime Minister. "My train didn't leave on time and then it went off in the wrong direction. It's chaos out there. What's going on?"

"It's the Sensible Tax, Sir," said one of his ministers. "Everyone is acting stupidly so that they don't have to pay it."

"Well, this can't go on," said the Prime Minister. "The country's gone mad."

"We shall have to stop the tax," someone said.

The Prime Minister paused. He liked the Sensible Tax; it raised lots of money. Without it the Treasury would be empty again. But things were getting out of hand.

"Yes," he said, sadly. And then he smiled. "I've got it," he cried. "Why don't we tax people for wearing clothes?"

All the ministers threw up their hands in complete despair.

"Oh no!" they groaned.

The Queen Who Hated Animals

When she was just a little girl, Princess Kalimena was bitten by one of her father's hunting dogs. Then she was scratched by the palace cat and one morning, while she was waiting for the groom to put her saddle in place, her horse stepped on her foot and bruised it badly. After that, Kalimena was scared of animals. As she grew, so her dislike of them grew until it was a fully grown hatred. If something had fur, feathers, claws, whiskers, fins or a tail, she hated it and would not allow it near her.

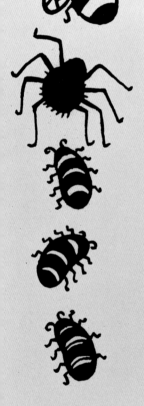

So when Princess Kalimena became Queen Kalimena, the first thing she did was pass a very unpopular new law.

"From this day forth, all animals are banned from the land," she declared.

Now this was not such a difficult thing to do in the palace grounds. The horses were removed from their stables, the dogs were taken out of their cosy kennels and the peacocks were banished from the gardens. But the servants in the palace had a terrible time. Spiders were brushed from the corners, shutters were closed against stray bees, but no matter what they did, woodlice always found a way in.

Out in the kingdom, it was even harder to banish the animals. The people needed their sheep and pigs, and their cows and chickens, and they loved their pets. What's more, how could they possibly banish the birds and snakes, butterflies and rabbits? It was a silly law made by a silly queen, they thought.

However, silly as she was, the Queen was very powerful and had to be obeyed. So the people found

a way round the problem. They kept the animals, but disguised them as other things so that the queen and her officials would never know they were still there.

One day, Queen Kalimena decided to take a tour of her land. She rumbled along the country lanes in her carriage, pulled very slowly by four very hot and tired guards.

"Can't you go any faster?" she yelled.

The queen waved to her subjects as they worked in the fields and she was pleased to see that there were no animals. However, some of the people did look very strange. Their clothes didn't fit them at all well and they didn't seem to be doing very much work. And once, when she was passing a hairy-looking scarecrow, she was convinced she heard it bleat like a goat.

When she became hungry, the queen stopped at the nearest house to have lunch. On this particular day, it was the house that belonged to Tasha and her family.

"The queen is coming," warned her father as he rushed into the house. "Are the animals hidden?"

"Yes," replied Tasha. "Just throw the tablecloth over the pig and we'll be ready."

"Now, stand very still," she said to the rabbits on the shelves who were pretending to be bookends. "And you two," she said to the cranes in the corner, "you're supposed to be lamps, remember, so no squawking."

The queen strode in haughtily.

"Your Majesty," said Tasha's mother, curtsying. "How lovely to see you."

"Oh, what a gorgeous shawl," said the queen, looking at two white swans that Tasha's father had hung on a peg with strict instructions not to flap their wings. The queen picked up the swans and draped them over her shoulders. "Oh, it fits me beautifully," she said. "So warm and surprisingly heavy."

She sat down.

Now, the chair that the queen sat in was really a kangaroo with a cloth thrown over him and when she sat down he did his best not to gasp or fidget. Tasha's mother put a wonderful display of food on the table, which was actually the pig, and the queen started to eat and drink.

Tasha and her mother and father watched nervously. Suddenly there was a bleating cry from outside and a thump. One of the sheep, which the farmers had put into the trees to make them look like low-lying clouds had fallen to the ground.

"What was that?" asked the queen, looking up from her meal.

"Oh, just the baby," said Tasha's mother. "He must have fallen out of his cot again. I'll go and put him back."

Just then, a hedgehog wandered out from under a chair and stopped in the middle of the floor.

"What is that?" asked the queen. "It looks like a hedge..."

"Oh, my brush," said Tasha. "I wondered where that had got to." And she picked up the hedgehog, turned it upside down and started brushing her hair with it. "I hate to have tangled hair, don't you, Your Majesty?"

"Indeed," said the queen, eyeing Tasha suspiciously. "Is there any pepper?" she asked.

"Here, Your Majesty," said Tasha, placing her pet hamster in front of the queen. Hammie was wearing a little hat full of pepper with holes in the top, and he was standing as still and upright as he could, with his eyes closed.

"What a strange-looking pepper pot," said the queen, picking up Hammie and shaking him vigorously. A cloud of pepper filled the room and Hammie sneezed.

"It sneezed!" cried the queen in alarm. "I am sure the pepper pot sneezed!"

Then one of the rabbits moved. It wasn't his fault; the heavy books were leaning against him. As books tumbled off the shelf the rabbit leapt out of the way to avoid being squashed.

The queen screamed and turned to Tasha, her face red with rage.

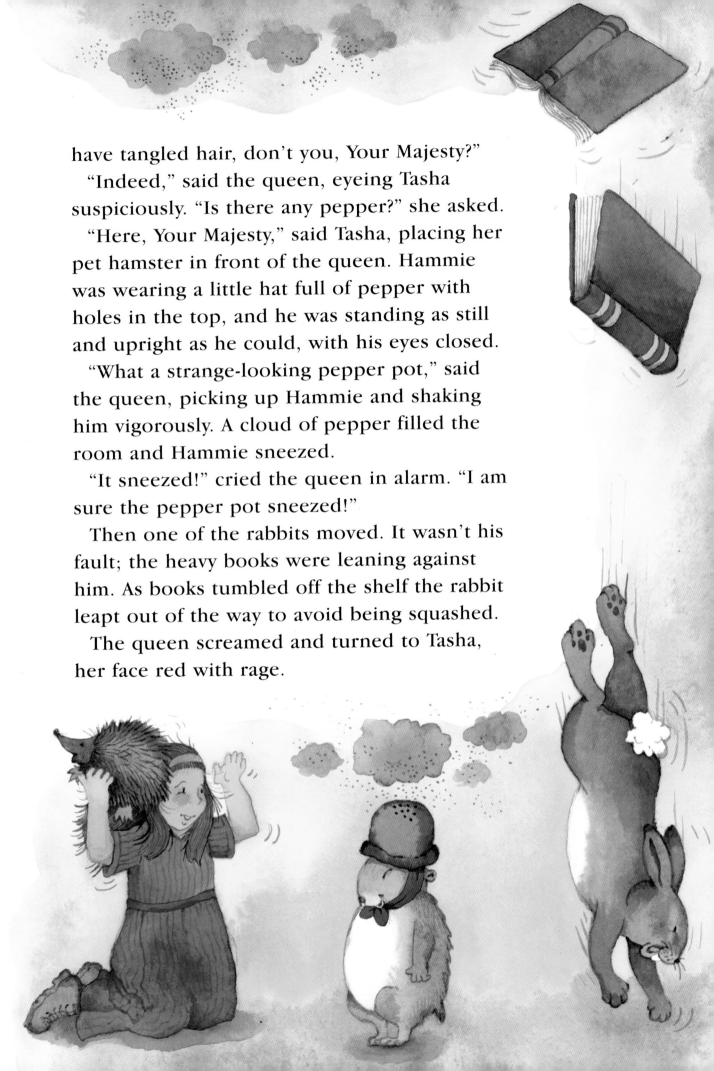

"You know I have banned animals!" she yelled, and stamped her foot hard, right on the kangaroo's foot. That was enough for the poor kangaroo. He started bounding around the room, with the queen clinging on for dear life. Squealing loudly, the pig ran off and the plates fell crashing to the floor. The cranes squawked and took off out of the window, the lampshades still on their heads. The cat cushions leapt from the chairs, the snake draught-excluders slithered out of the door and the kangaroo bounded out of the house and made for the open country, with Queen Kalimena still clinging on.

"Put me down!" screamed the queen, and finally the kangaroo did – but just then the swans decided it was time to get away.

They flapped their wings and took to the

air, taking the queen with them as they flew. Higher and higher they soared.

"OHHH!" screamed the queen. Then "Oohh," in a slightly different voice. She was flying, which was something she'd always wanted to do. The swans took her high over her kingdom, beating their great white wings and the queen laughed as she swooped low over the palace and the town. When the swans finally brought the queen gently down beside the lake, she was ecstatic with joy.

Her court officials ran outside.

"Shoot the swans," one of them shouted.

"No," cried the queen. "Let them live. Let all the animals live. They are wonderful."

So the swans returned to the lake, the rabbits went back to their burrows, the sheep climbed gratefully down from the trees, and they all lived properly ever after.

The Flying Contest

It was a hot day on the African savannah when the animals saw that a notice had been pinned to the trunk of a tree. They gathered around to read it.

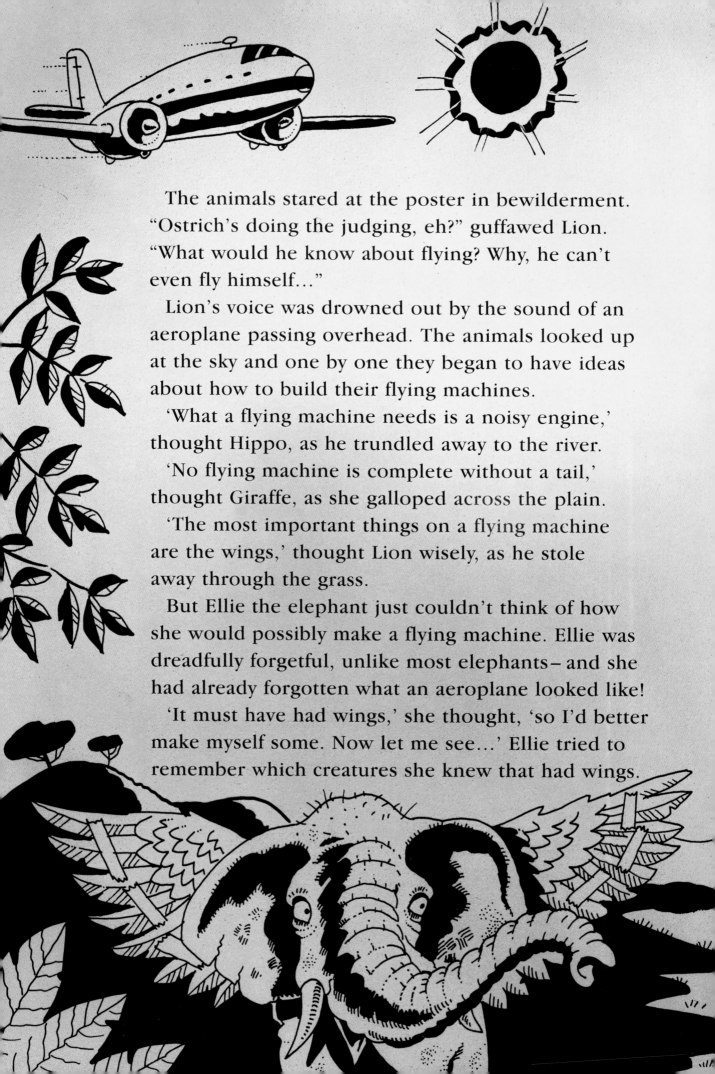

The animals stared at the poster in bewilderment. "Ostrich's doing the judging, eh?" guffawed Lion. "What would he know about flying? Why, he can't even fly himself…"

Lion's voice was drowned out by the sound of an aeroplane passing overhead. The animals looked up at the sky and one by one they began to have ideas about how to build their flying machines.

'What a flying machine needs is a noisy engine,' thought Hippo, as he trundled away to the river.

'No flying machine is complete without a tail,' thought Giraffe, as she galloped across the plain.

'The most important things on a flying machine are the wings,' thought Lion wisely, as he stole away through the grass.

But Ellie the elephant just couldn't think of how she would possibly make a flying machine. Ellie was dreadfully forgetful, unlike most elephants– and she had already forgotten what an aeroplane looked like!

'It must have had wings,' she thought, 'so I'd better make myself some. Now let me see…' Ellie tried to remember which creatures she knew that had wings.

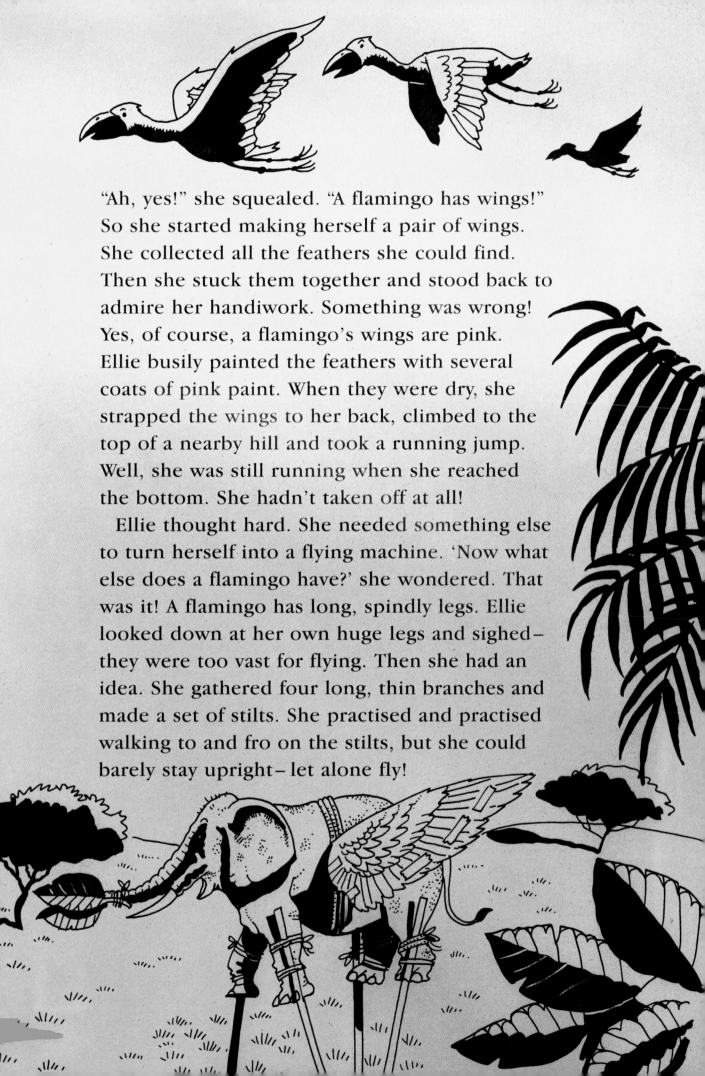

"Ah, yes!" she squealed. "A flamingo has wings!"
So she started making herself a pair of wings.
She collected all the feathers she could find.
Then she stuck them together and stood back to
admire her handiwork. Something was wrong!
Yes, of course, a flamingo's wings are pink.
Ellie busily painted the feathers with several
coats of pink paint. When they were dry, she
strapped the wings to her back, climbed to the
top of a nearby hill and took a running jump.
Well, she was still running when she reached
the bottom. She hadn't taken off at all!

Ellie thought hard. She needed something else
to turn herself into a flying machine. 'Now what
else does a flamingo have?' she wondered. That
was it! A flamingo has long, spindly legs. Ellie
looked down at her own huge legs and sighed –
they were too vast for flying. Then she had an
idea. She gathered four long, thin branches and
made a set of stilts. She practised and practised
walking to and fro on the stilts, but she could
barely stay upright – let alone fly!

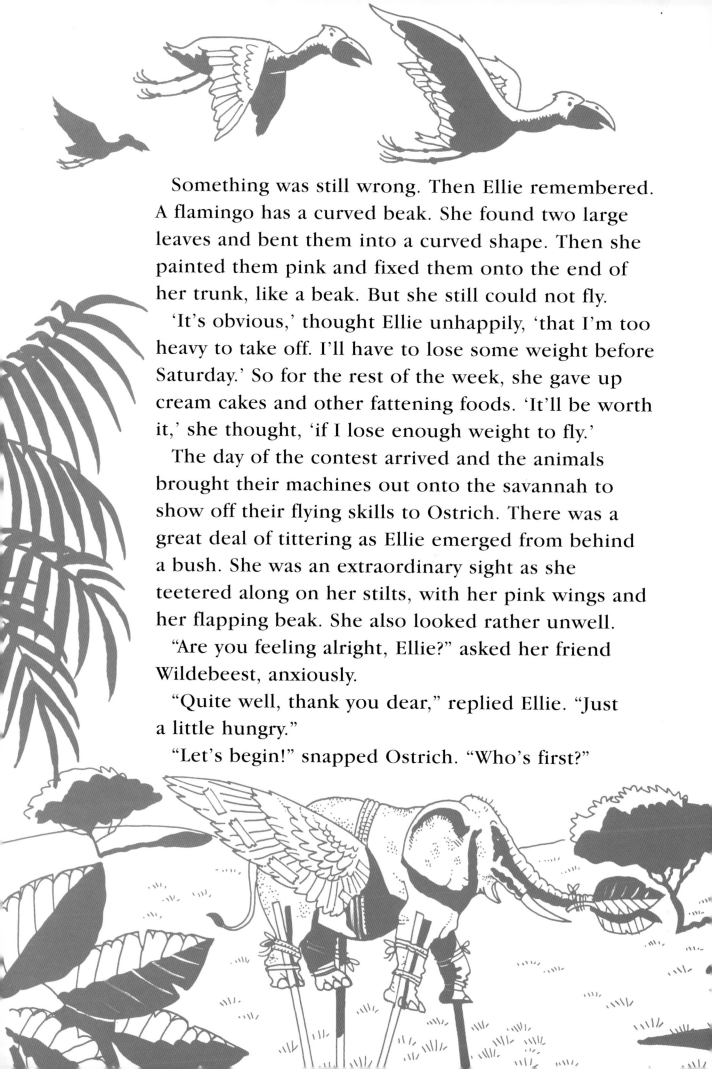

Something was still wrong. Then Ellie remembered. A flamingo has a curved beak. She found two large leaves and bent them into a curved shape. Then she painted them pink and fixed them onto the end of her trunk, like a beak. But she still could not fly.

'It's obvious,' thought Ellie unhappily, 'that I'm too heavy to take off. I'll have to lose some weight before Saturday.' So for the rest of the week, she gave up cream cakes and other fattening foods. 'It'll be worth it,' she thought, 'if I lose enough weight to fly.'

The day of the contest arrived and the animals brought their machines out onto the savannah to show off their flying skills to Ostrich. There was a great deal of tittering as Ellie emerged from behind a bush. She was an extraordinary sight as she teetered along on her stilts, with her pink wings and her flapping beak. She also looked rather unwell.

"Are you feeling alright, Ellie?" asked her friend Wildebeest, anxiously.

"Quite well, thank you dear," replied Ellie. "Just a little hungry."

"Let's begin!" snapped Ostrich. "Who's first?"

"I am!" cried Hippo, leaping into the seat of his machine. "What a flying machine needs is noise!" he shouted over the roar of the engine. It really was a magnificent machine. It looked a bit like a lawn mower with huge, shiny pistons.

"Isn't there something missing?" mused Cheetah with a smile.

But Hippo wasn't listening. "Here we go!" he cried, letting out the throttle as the machine shot off across the savannah in a cloud of black smoke. Faster and faster went the machine. but it didn't take off, of course, because it had no wings.

"Ha, ha!" laughed the animals with glee, as it smashed into a tree and Hippo climbed out looking disgruntled.

"Who's next?" asked Ostrich.

"Oh, I am," said Giraffe. "What a flying machine really needs is a tail," she said, as she climbed into her machine. It was spectacular, with a gleaming metal tail standing proudly at the back. She cantered off across the savannah, four legs sticking out of the machine. Faster and faster she galloped, but she didn't take off, because it had no wings.

"Hee, hee!" giggled the animals, as Giraffe's legs got all tangled up and she collapsed in a dizzy heap.

"Who's next?" said Ostrich.

"Meee!" purred Lion smugly. "You foolish animals," he sneered. "What a flying machine needs is wings." And he leaped effortlessly into his machine. The animals gasped in awe. Lion's machine had a simply beautiful pair of silver wings stretching out on either side.

Faster and faster went Lion across the savannah and it looked as if his machine really might take off. He gave a great roar of triumph and a fly flew into his gaping mouth. He coughed, lost control and the machine careered off course and into a watering hole.

"Ha, ha, hee, hee!" bellowed the animals, as a very wet Lion crawled out of the water.

"Now, what about Ellie?" said Ostrich, wiping tears of mirth from his eyes. But Ellie was nowhere to be found. When she had seen the other animals' machines she had been so ashamed of her own efforts that she had crept away. Besides, she was feeling very hungry.

'I'll have a nice picnic on my own,' she thought. She wrapped all her favourite foods in a tablecloth, tied it with string and set off to find a quiet spot. She was munching a delicious jam doughnut when suddenly there was a tremendous gust of wind. Before she

could escape, she felt herself being lifted up in the tablecloth and carried high above the trees. She struggled to free herself and got all tangled up in the string.

Just then, the other animals felt the gust too. They looked up into the sky and stared in amazement. They couldn't believe their eyes! Ellie was floating down towards them with the tablecloth and string acting as a parachute!

"Ellie, you're the winner!" announced Ostrich, as she landed on the ground with a soft bump. The other animals cheered and cheered. "It's time to claim your prize – bring out the balloon basket!" called Ostrich. Ellie tried to squeeze her large frame into the basket, but it simply wouldn't fit.

"I'd miss you all anyway," she said. "Why don't we have a picnic together instead? I'm still hungry, as it happens!" So that is exactly what they all did.

The Dog who Couldn't Bark

Ben gazed into a pair of large brown eyes, and the large brown eyes gazed back. It was a good face, friendly and intelligent, the sort of face that promised fun. Ben liked it immediately. Even though there were seven puppies to choose from, Ben knew that the little brown-and-white one with the funny ears and the curly tail was the one for him.

The puppy began to chase round and round in circles; then he rolled over a couple of times as Ben looked on in amusement and admiration.

"I think I like this one best," announced Ben as the puppy grabbed the sleeve of his jacket and began to tug at it playfully. Ben's dad frowned. As well as being by far the smallest in the litter, the puppy had a floppy ear that fell over his eye whilst the other stuck straight up in the air. And his tail curled round and round, just like a pig's. "He's rather small," Ben's dad pointed out, and the little puppy doubled his height by standing on his back legs and springing around the kitchen as if he were on a pogo stick.

"Please…" said Ben, as the puppy jumped up and tried to nibble his nose.

"Oh very well," agreed Ben's dad, seeing that the two were already inseparable. "But he has to be a guard dog not just a pet."

The puppy bared his teeth and made the most fearsome and ferocious face he could.

"Oh look," said Ben, giggling. "He's smiling."

"Has he got a good bark?" asked Ben's dad,

writing out a cheque and handing it over to Mrs Walker, the lady selling the pups. She smiled broadly. "Well that's the oddest thing, he doesn't bark at all. I don't think he can."

Ben's dad was still shaking his head by the time the three of them arrived home.

"A six-inch high guard dog, with a ridiculous tail, a floppy ear and no bark," he complained to Ben's mum as she watched Ben and his new best friend race around the garden.

"Well, Ben certainly seems to like him," she remarked. And Ben certainly did.

It didn't take long for the new puppy to settle in. Ben gave him the name Jake, which sort of suited him. Jake was having the time of his life, a splendid new basket, a smart tartan collar with his name on it, an enormous garden and a wonderful family. He tried very hard to please them all, in particular Ben's dad. He handed him the hammer when he was fixing the *Beware of the Dog* sign to the gate. He hadn't meant to drop it on his toe of course, but it was rather heavy for a small dog.

He also helped in the garden doing a lot of digging and rearranging the flower beds. After that Ben's dad had been so delighted that he had shut Jake in the back porch so he could have a lovely long rest in his basket– digging was hard work, especially when you only had short legs.

And Jake did so love his basket. But, as the weeks rolled by and winter approached, it occurred to him that he might be warmer and even more comfortable if he took his splendid grey blanket and laid it on the sofa in the lounge– after all Ben's dad spent many a happy hour there.

It wasn't easy dragging the heavy blanket down the hall but eventually he managed just in time to see two men climbing in through the lounge window.

"'Ere, they've got a dog," said the first man, whose name was Stan, as he shone a torch in Jake's bewildered face.

"That would explain the sign on the gate," replied the second man, whose name was Eric, as he tumbled headfirst through the window.

"What sign?" asked Stan, who could not read.

"The one that said *Beware of the Dog*," said Eric, putting his cap back on his head.

"Nice doggie, good doggie," began Stan. He approached Jake, who cocked his head to one side and wagged his tail.

"It's okay, he's friendly," said Stan. Eric tiptoed over, but didn't see Jake's blanket strewn across the middle of the floor and fell flat on his face. Jake licked his ear. "Geroff," said Eric, trying not to laugh even though he was rather ticklish.

"Shhh," Stan said, and then pointed to a cabinet in the corner of the room. "The family silver," he added, rubbing his gloved hands together. Jake stared inquisitively at the two men. They looked rather odd in their stripy jumpers and the peculiar masks that covered their eyes. He wanted to bark, but of course he couldn't, so he just watched as both men began to fill a large sack with Ben's dad's golf trophies. Jake instinctively knew that this wasn't right, strangers tiptoeing about in the middle of the night helping themselves to whatever they fancied. He ran towards Stan and grabbed the seat of his trousers firmly in his teeth. "Get 'im off me," said Stan in a loud whisper, but Jake would not let go. Eric grabbed the dog by his back legs and pulled and pulled until there was a rrrrr**rrrrip**.

Stan's trousers tore to reveal a pair of red and white spotted boxer shorts. Eric landed with a loud thud on the floor.

"Shhhhh…" said Stan rather too loudly, but upstairs no-one stirred.

Jake ran round and round in circles. He knew he had to make a noise, so he opened his mouth to bark, but all that came out was a weak little whimper. Then everything went black as Stan threw the blanket over him.

Jake wriggled and squirmed and squirmed and wriggled until he saw a scrap of light appear. Then he wriggled towards it until his nose peeped out.

"Up there," said Stan pointing to the top of the piano. Just as Eric grasped the magnificent silver candelabra, Jake leapt onto the piano stool and then onto the piano trotting up and down the keys and creating the loudest and most terrible noise imaginable. Within seconds every light in the house seemed to be switched on and the sound of footsteps could be heard on the stairs.

"Run," shouted Eric, dropping the candelabra and the contents of the sack on the floor and

the two men fled through the open window.

When Ben's dad opened the lounge door, he couldn't believe his eyes. The sack lay discarded on the floor with all his prized golf trophies spilling out of it, while little Jake ran up and down the piano keys wagging his curly tail frantically.

Ben and his mum came into the room. "What on earth happened in here?" asked Ben's mum, looking worried.

"It seems we had intruders," explained Ben's dad. He walked over to Jake and scratched him behind his ears. "But our guard dog here raised the alarm." Ben and his mum ran over to congratulate the clever, courageous little puppy and Jake played an encore, dancing up and down the keys until everyone was laughing, holding onto their ears and begging him to stop.

"I think," began Ben's dad lifting Jake down, "I prefer Bach!"